HERE COMES HERCULES!

✦

STELLA TARAKSON

Sweet Cherry
Publishing

Published by Sweet Cherry Publishing Limited
Unit 36, Vulcan House,
Vulcan Road,
Leicester, LE5 3EF,
United Kingdom

First published in the UK in 2017
2018 edition

ISBN: 978-1-78226-355-5

Cover Design by Nick Roberts and Rhiannon Izard
Illustrations by Nick Roberts

www.sweetcherrypublishing.com

Printed and bound in Great Britain by

In memory of my father Constantine,
a real Greek hero

The tiger lay at Tim Baker's feet with its mouth wide open. Its striped fur was grimy and tattered, as if it had fought in many fights. Its lips were drawn back in a snarl. Pointy yellow teeth gleamed in the fading light. They looked very sharp.

Tim felt the sweat trickle down his face. He wiped it away with the back of his hand. He had to keep going. The day was nearly over, but there was still a lot to do.

It was hot and humid and he could hear the rumble of distant thunder. The storm was getting nearer. Not looking where he was going, Tim shuffled forward. He stepped closer to the tiger, who watched and waited in silence.

Tim's foot landed centimetres from its head.

'Sorry,' he said, edging around the massive beast. He was careful not to tread on its outstretched paws.

The tiger gazed back at him through glassy eyes. It looked like it wanted to leap up and growl. Instead it lay silent and still, poised as if ready to pounce. Tim bent down and patted its furry head. A cloud of dust flew out, which made him sneeze.

'Wow, you're dirty! Guess I'll have to clean you, too. But not now. I gotta dust before Mum comes home.'

The tiger said nothing. It lay on the living room floor, watching Tim hunt reluctantly for the duster.

Tim often spoke to the tiger-skin rug. It kept him company after school, while Mum was at her second job. Mum worked in an office during the day, then as a cleaner in the evening. She worked from early in the morning until dinner time. Mum didn't like being away from home for such long hours, but she had no choice. They needed the money.

Which meant Tim had to help out at home. Everyone had to pull their weight, Mum said. Tim tried. It didn't mean he had to like it.

He found the duster crammed under the sofa, where he'd left it the last time he had done the dusting. Sighing, he pulled it out and turned to the mantelpiece.

First the crystal skull, then the wooden elephant. Tim's house was full of things his parents had collected from overseas. Rugs, statues, paintings … It was like living in a museum. A reminder of better times, the jumbled collection now sat around gathering dust.

Tim moved on to the old Greek vase. It was big and black, with a narrow neck and two curved handles. Two black figures stood out on a clay-coloured panel: a muscleman wrestling a fierce bull. The bull was bigger, but it looked like the man was winning.

'You know what?' Tim said to the tiger, taking a break from cleaning. 'That bull looks familiar. Weird. I don't think I've met any bulls lately.' He raked a hand through his mop of curly brown hair as he examined the picture closely. That wiry red hair, the stocky build, the angry face …

Tim jumped. That was it! The bull looked like Leo. Just as cross and just as stupid. If his worst enemy had horns, Leo and the bull would be twins. 'I guess that's why they're called bullies,' Tim muttered. 'They look like bulls.'

He wondered how on earth the man could be defeating the animal. It was twice his size and pure, solid muscle. But the man looked like he was used to adventures and heroic feats. He probably wasn't stuck at home doing housework all the time. And the bull almost certainly didn't call him Cinderella!

Tim whipped the duster about roughly. Everyone thought the nickname Leo had invented for him was funny. Everyone except Tim. The vase wobbled alarmingly and started to topple. Steadying it with both hands, he gazed at the jagged writing on the vase. He wished he could read it. It might explain the man's secret. It might tell him how to defeat Leo.

'One day, I'll learn to read the words. I'll tell you what they mean,' Tim told the tiger-skin rug.

The tiger looked back blankly.

'Hey, it's not easy! Even Mum can't read it. It's in Greek. The alphabet's different.'

The tiger said nothing. It didn't believe him.

'I can read some of it.' Tim gripped the vase carefully, the way his mother had shown him, and tilted it so he could see better. 'That's an E and that looks like–'

Just then, the phone rang. Startled, Tim jerked backwards, his fingers still looped around the handles.

CRASH!

The vase toppled to the floor, smashing into bits. Tim's heart beat faster. Mum would go nuts if she found out. He had to fix it, quickly, before she came home.

14

The phone kept ringing. Tim leapt over the pieces of broken vase to answer it.

'Hello?'

'Hi darling.' It was Mum. 'Just letting you know I'm stuck in traffic. I'll be a bit late.'

Tim's mind raced as he tried to remember where he'd put the superglue. 'Good. I mean … okay.'

Mum paused. 'Is everything all right?'

'Yeah. I'm dusting, that's all.'

'You're a good boy.' Mum sighed. 'One day, things will be different. I promise. I won't have to work long hours forever.'

'I know.' Tim eyed the broken pieces anxiously.

The Greek vase was the only thing in the house that was worth any money. It was very, very old – thousands of years – and that made it valuable. Sometimes Mum talked about selling it. It would bring in enough money for her to quit her second job, giving her more time at home with Tim. She could never bring herself to do it, however: the vase was the last thing Dad had given her before he died.

And now it was smashed. Scattered in

pieces across the living room floor.

And it was all Tim's fault.

'Gotta go,' he chirped, trying to sound as if nothing were wrong. 'See you soon!'

Tim scrambled around on his hands and knees, gathering chunks of vase. It wasn't too bad, he decided, fitting two bits together. With a bit of luck, he could fix it so it was as good as new and Mum would never know.

'FREE AT LAST!'

a voice boomed.

Tim nearly dropped the pieces. He looked up.

And up.

And up.

An enormous man loomed above him. His legs were like tree trunks and his shoulders were as broad as the coffee table. He wore a grey garment fastened on one shoulder, exposing a muscular and hairy chest. A thick brown belt encircled his waist and his feet were thrust into the largest sandals Tim had ever seen.

'Who – who are you?' Tim's voice shook.

'Do not be afraid,' the muscleman said. 'I was a prisoner in the vase. You broke it and set me free.' With a hand the size of a dinner plate, he helped Tim gently up to his feet.

Tim's knees had gone all wobbly. This couldn't be happening! He stared at the man in disbelief.

'How did you get in there? You're far too big.'

'I was trapped by the wicked Hera.' The man planted his fists on his hips and twisted his spine until it cracked. 'Ah, that's better. It was cramped in there. Hot, too.'

'Hang on, what did you say? The wicked who?'

'Hera. The foulest, most evil woman in the world. She is so terrible, even the rocks tremble as she passes. Don't you know her?' The muscleman's eyebrows shot up in surprise.

Tim shook his head. 'Not me, sorry.'

'And who are you, exactly?'

'Tim Baker.'

An enthusiastic smile crept across the muscleman's face. 'You're a baker?

EXCELLENT.'

He rubbed his hands together. 'I'm starving. Give me two large white loaves, extra crunchy crust.'

'No, I–'

'A small wholemeal?'

'Baker's my name, not my job. I don't have a job. I'm ten.'

The man sniffed. 'You don't have a job. You haven't heard of Hera. Are you perhaps of feeble mind?'

'No kid has a job!'

'Really? I suppose I have been trapped a long time,' the man admitted, stroking his wiry black beard. 'Then I shall try to explain: Hera is the queen goddess, wife of my father Zeus. You've heard of the mighty Zeus, at least?'

Tim had come across that name before. Frowning, he tried to remember where. Was it in a cartoon?

A book? Some sort of story, he was sure of that.

'My father is lord of the sky and ruler of Mount Olympus,' the man said, pulling himself to his full height. 'You must know of him.'

'Mount Olympus? Like in mythology? Greek gods and stuff?' Tim clicked his tongue. 'They're just stories. They're not real.'

The man lowered his bushy eyebrows as he peered down at Tim. 'Not real?' he echoed, sounding displeased. 'Of course they are. They're as real as me, and I am a demigod – half god, half human. Are you of poor vision? Do you doubt your own eyes?'

Tim couldn't argue with that. He said nothing.

'Queen Hera has hated me since I was born,' the man continued, clenching his fists. 'When I was only a few days old, she sent snakes into my cot to kill me. But I showed her: I seized the snakes and strangled them with my bare hands.'

Tim felt the blood drain from his face. What sort of person would do that to a baby?

'Wh-why does she hate you?'

'She's jealous of my mother, who is far more beautiful than her. Hera never forgets an insult ... and she never forgives. She trapped me in that cursed vase, snatching me from my beloved wife and daughter. Now, thanks to you, the spell is broken.'

'Spell?' Tim thought for a moment. If this were really happening ... if he weren't imagining things ... did that mean what he thought it meant? A wide grin broke out on his face. 'Hey, are you a genie? Are you going to grant me three wishes?'

'A GENIE?'

The muscleman's voice boomed across the room, rattling the windows in their frames and making Tim wince. 'Do I look like a genie?'

Tim peered at the muscleman. He wasn't exactly sure what a genie was meant to look like.

'I think so,' he said. 'Except for the dress.'

'It is not a dress! It's a chiton.'

The man tugged at his short tunic.

Tim held out a piece of vase. 'Genie, fix this so that it's as good as new. That's wish number one. Number two – make Leo leave me alone. And wish number three – I wish I didn't have to clean up all the time.'

'Stop calling me that. I am not a genie.' The man glared at him.

'Oh.' That meant no wishes, Tim realised with dismay. 'Then what are you?'

'I am a hero, the bravest and mightiest of them all. You must have heard of me: my name is Hercules.'

Tim jumped. A real live superhero, right here in his house! That was nearly as good as a genie.

'Cool! What do you do? Can you fly?' he asked eagerly.

'No.'

'Can you shoot spiderwebs out of your wrists?'

Hercules frowned and shook his head.

'Can you shoot laser beams out of your eyes?'

Hercules folded his arms across his chest and looked grumpily back at Tim.

'Well then, what *can* you do?' Tim asked. 'What sort of hero are you?'

'I can do lots of things,' Hercules said. 'Like this.' He grunted and flexed his arm muscles. They bulged like volcanoes about to erupt.

'Yes ... and?'

'And this!'

Hercules lifted the sofa and raised it over his head. The wooden armrests bumped against the ceiling, leaving deep scratch marks.

'That's good,' Tim said, nodding. 'Can you stick this vase back together?'

Hercules let the sofa drop into place. It fell with a clatter. He peered at the pieces of vase scattered on the floor. Squatting down, he prodded them with fingers the size of sausages.

'I don't think so,' he said. 'The bits are too small. I can't pick them up with these super-strong fingers.'

Tim sighed. 'I'll fix it later.' He scooped up the pieces and shoved them in a drawer, out of sight. With luck, Mum wouldn't notice that the vase was missing before he had a chance to repair it.

'Heroes don't fix pots,' Hercules said scornfully. 'When I was your age, I wrestled a cow with my bare hands. Have you ever wrestled a cow?'

'Um, no.' Tim was trying to be polite, but didn't see how any of this would help. Flexing muscles and wrestling cattle wouldn't get the housework done.

'Cows, hmmm. That reminds me. I haven't eaten for thousands of years. Do you have any food? I'm starving.'

Tim led the hero into the kitchen. Hercules sat on a cane chair. It creaked and strained under his weight. Tim opened the fridge door and peered inside. 'There's some leftover roast chicken. Would you like some?'

Hercules didn't bother to answer. As soon as Tim put the platter down, the hero fell upon the chicken, slurping and chewing.

Within seconds, all that was left was bones. Burping, he wiped his mouth on the back of his hand.

Tim watched silently then cleared up the mess. Heroes may be cool, but he couldn't help thinking a genie would be more useful.

'Thank you, Tim Baker. Heroes need food to stay strong,' Hercules said, patting his stomach. 'That was a good meal. How did you get the drumsticks so tender?'

But Tim was more concerned about his wishes.

'If you're not a genie, does that mean you can't help me?' he asked.

Hercules licked his fingers and looked thoughtful. 'I can't fix the pot. I don't know who this Leo is and why he must leave you alone. But as for your third wish … Yes, I,

THE MIGHTY HERCULES,

shall help you with the cleaning.'

Tim brightened. Maybe heroes were useful after all! 'Can you weed gardens?' he asked, thinking of all the jobs he still had to do that day.

'Weed? What is that?'

'It means you pull out the weeds – the bad plants. If you don't, they take over and kill the good plants.'

'Kill, you say?' Hercules' eyebrows shot up. 'Worry not. I shall save them! That's what we heroes do. Show me these evil plants at once.'

Tim led Hercules out the front door. He pointed out yellow dandelion flowers and white clover blossoms. They nestled amongst the blades of grass and peeked out of the flower beds. 'Those are weeds. We only remove the bad plants. Nothing else.'

'It shall be done,' Hercules said, locking his fingers together and cracking his knuckles. 'Stand back, my friend. This might be dangerous. I don't want you to get hurt.'

'It's easier to take out the weeds if you use this.' Tim picked up a small spade and handed it to the hero.

Eyes shining, Hercules took it. He made slashing motions in the air.

'Dig the weeds out from the roots,' Tim said, 'so they don't regrow.'

Hercules threw himself on the grass, flat on his stomach. He stuck his nose near a dandelion and snarled at it. 'Killing the good

plants, ay? I'll soon stop you!' He lashed out
with the spade. He lopped the head off one
dandelion, then another.

'NOT LIKE THAT!'

Tim shouted, alarmed. 'That just spreads the weeds. You end up with more.'

Hercules ignored him. He leapt to his feet. At super-speed, the hero darted around the garden. Ducking and bobbing, lopping the heads off all the weeds.

'How was that?' Hercules said when he came to a halt. 'Are you not amazed by my strength and agility?'

Tim looked at the decapitated blossoms strewn across the garden. It would take forever to clear them up. Now he had even more work to do. He frowned.

'What's wrong?' Hercules asked, looking offended. 'Are you not pleased? I did as you asked. You saw me destroy the wicked weeds.'

'Ye-e-s …' Tim didn't want to hurt the hero's feelings. After all, he was only trying to help. 'But that only makes them come back faster.'

Hercules thrust out a huge hand, gripping Tim hard above the elbow. 'You're right, my friend! I think they're growing back already. They must be like the many-headed Hydra. Every time you chopped a head off, it would grow right back.'

'The what?' Tim asked, rubbing his arm.

'Hydra. A monstrous serpent with heads like giant snakes. It was so venomous, even its breath could kill. Hera created it purely so that it would destroy me.'

Tim gaped. This Hera must have been truly awful.

'Do you want to know how I defeated it? I will tell you! First I covered my nose and mouth to protect myself from its foul breath.' Hercules demonstrated with his free hand. 'Then I cut off all of its heads as fast as I could.'

With a yell, Hercules charged around the garden again, slashing and ripping with the spade. This time, he sliced up all the flowers too. Roses, daisies, petunias.

'No, no!' Tim ran behind him, waving his arms and shouting. Hercules didn't listen. He kept on slicing until there were no flowers left.

Panting, Hercules came to a standstill. He gazed proudly across the lawn. 'Then I made my brilliant discovery. There is only one sure way to stop the Hydra heads from returning. Fire! Burn the neck stumps and the heads can't grow back.'

The hero reached into his tunic and pulled out a small, grey rock. He scraped it with a sharp fingernail until a small flame emerged.

'No!' Tim yelped, guessing what was about to happen.

'STOP!'

'Don't worry, I'll stop the Hydra weeds,' Hercules said, setting a dry branch alight. He lifted the flaming torch to the sky. 'Because I'm a hero!'

Before Tim could stop him, Hercules took off. Racing around the garden, the hero seared all the plant stems with the burning torch. He burnt weeds and flowers alike. Soon all that was left was a blackened, smoking mess. Small flames erupted here and there and Tim chased after them, kicking up clods of dirt to put them out.

Hercules extinguished the torch with a flourish.

'There! I have saved your garden. No, don't thank me. That's what heroes are for.'

'Saved it? You've ruined it! How am I ever going to explain …?' The words died in Tim's throat as Mum's car pulled up.

Still wearing her cleaner's uniform, Mum climbed out of the car. She looked tired. Her shoulders were slumped and she was walking slowly. When she saw the smouldering garden, however, she

rushed to the gate. Her eyes
bulged.

'Tim! Are you all right?' She
gripped him by the shoulders.
'What on earth happened?'

'You know the difference between make-believe and the truth, don't you?' Mum asked.

Tim and Mum were sitting at the kitchen table. It was time for dinner. Tim was very hungry but Mum wanted to talk.

'Yes. I'm telling you the truth.'

'I'm not angry.' Mum was using her patient voice. She reached out and held Tim's hand. 'Why did you burn the garden? Tell me what's upsetting you.'

'Nothing. I keep telling you. I didn't burn anything.'

Mum tried again. 'I know you don't like cleaning. And I know you get lonely after school.'

'It's not that,' Tim said, his freckled nose twitching with emotion. He had told Mum everything. Everything … except for the bit about breaking the vase. It was still in the drawer, where it would stay hidden until Tim found a chance to fix it.

He'd explained that an Ancient Greek hero had suddenly appeared in the living room and offered to help with the housework. The hero didn't know much about weeding and was only doing what

he thought was right. Mum didn't believe
Tim. She thought he had made Hercules
up.

'But, but, he's here. Can't you see? In
that chair.' Tim pointed.

Mum looked through Hercules as if
he weren't there. 'That's enough.' She
was starting to sound cross. 'Imagination
is good but you're taking it too far,
Timothy.'

Mum only called him that
when she was angry.

Tim looked helplessly across the table.

'You can see me,' the hero said, 'because you set me free. No one else can see or hear me.'

'This is terrible,' Tim said. What was the point of an invisible hero? Who would believe him?

'Don't worry.' Mum thought Tim was talking to her. 'I know what the problem is. You're lonely. You're upset because I'm away all day.'

'That's not–'

Mum patted his cheek distractedly and kept talking. 'One day I'll get promoted at my office job. One day a publisher will like my stories and make them into books. And, eventually, we'll have enough money for

me to quit my second job. Then I'll be able
to spend more time at home with you.'

Hercules sniffed. He wiped a tear from
his eye. 'That's so sad. I know how your
mother feels. I miss my family too: I wish
I could be at home with them. I hope
your mother succeeds in her honourable
quest.'

'Mum'll make it,' Tim whispered. 'She
writes great stories.'

Mum leaned over and gave Tim a quick
hug.

'Thank you for believing in me. It helps.'
Sighing, she stood and trudged over to the
fridge. 'It's time to eat. I'm glad we've got
leftover chicken. I'm too tired to cook.'

'Ah …'

Mum spun around, her long ponytail flying. 'Where is it? Did you eat it? How did you eat it all? It was almost a

WHOLE CHICKEN!'

'Hercules ate it. Heroes get hungry.'

Mum stared at Tim. He could tell she was trying not to lose her temper. Her cheeks turned red and her back stiffened. 'I guess you won't want any dinner, not after eating all of that.'

'But I'm starving! I haven't eaten anything. Honest.'

'I don't feel like cooking. We'll have salad.'

Tim's shoulders drooped. He hated salad.

Hercules burped and smiled. It was the sort of smile people have when they're full of roast chicken. Tim's stomach growled unhappily as Mum sliced tomatoes and cucumbers and piled them high on their plates.

■　■　■

The next morning, Mum drank her coffee and ran out the front door.

'Bye, dear. See you tonight!' She was in a hurry as usual.

Loud snoring drifted out from the living room. Tim stuck his head through the doorway. Hercules was fast asleep on the sofa, mouth open, long legs dangling over the armrest. Tim tiptoed past. He didn't want to wake him. Heroes needed their sleep.

Tim decided to do some cleaning now, early in the day, so there'd be less to do later.

'Where should I start?' Then he remembered. The tiger-skin rug. It was very dusty.

The rug was heavier than he'd expected. Tim gripped the tiger's ears with both hands and then heaved. He dragged it down the hall and out the back door. Getting it onto the clothes line took all of his strength. He pulled and tugged and hauled. Finally, the stuffed head flopped over the line. The tiger snarled silently and its eyes bulged.

'Don't worry, this won't hurt a bit,' Tim said. 'Soon have you good as new.'

He fastened some pegs on the tiger's fur to stop it from sliding off. He shook it. A cloud of dust flew out, making him sneeze. He needed something to hit the rug with. 'Hang on. I'll get my cricket bat.'

The tiger didn't reply. It hung patiently on the clothes line, staring across the lawn, and down towards the creek that bubbled and tumbled noisily through the bottom of the garden. Tim ran into the shed and fetched his bat. When he returned, Hercules was standing at the back door, stretching and yawning.

'Good morning,' Tim said. 'How'd you sleep?'

Hercules ran his hands through his hair. 'Not very well. Your sofa is too …'

Tim didn't find out what was wrong
with the sofa, however, because Hercules
suddenly gave a loud yell.

'BEWARE! A TIGER!

A vicious, man-eating tiger. Right behind
you!'

'No, it's just–'

Pausing only to flex his muscles, the
hero rushed to Tim's side. 'Do not fear,
Tim Baker, the mighty Hercules will save
you!'

'You don't need to save me,' Tim said,
prodding the tiger-skin rug with the
cricket bat. 'It's not dangerous, it's just
a rug.'

'Don't you believe it. Once a man-eater,
always a man-eater. And you, my friend,
are snack-sized.'

Hercules pulled the bat out of Tim's
hands. He poked at the stuffed head. The
rug swayed back and forth on the clothes

line. 'See how it threatens us? It prepares to pounce.'

'But it's dead.'

'That's what it wants you to think.' Hercules growled at the tiger. 'You can't fool me, vile beast.'

Tim took his bat back and put it down a safe distance away. 'It's just a–' he started to say.

'Hah!'

Tim looked on, horrified, as Hercules dragged the tiger skin to the ground. The hero and the rug rolled around and around the backyard. One moment Hercules was on top, the next moment the rug was. Soil and bits of grass clung to the tiger skin. It was dirtier than ever.

As they tussled, Hercules glared at the tiger's jaws. 'I've beaten mightier foes than you. Even the Lion of Nemea, the most fearsome beast in the world.'

The tiger didn't answer. It flopped bonelessly as Hercules kept on rolling and talking.

'That ugly cat was a man-eater. Its hide was so thick, no weapon could pierce it. I was the only one strong enough to defeat it. Do you want to know how I did it?'

The tiger's head nodded limply.

'Don't try making friends with me,' Hercules hissed. 'You don't fool me that easily.' With one powerful leap, Hercules flipped them both over so that the skin was pinned beneath his knees.

'I didn't need a weapon,' Hercules continued, scowling into the tiger's face. 'I killed it with my bare hands, then I cut through its skin with its own sharp claws. And guess what? I turned that tough lion into a cloak. I'd give up now if I were you.'

Suddenly, there was a loud ripping sound. A long tear appeared in the tiger-skin rug, all the way from its tail to its front paw.

'That's more like it.' Jumping to his feet, Hercules slapped the dirt off his hands. 'Victory is mine!'

Tim groaned. How was he going to fix the rug without Mum finding out? After the fiasco with the garden, she'd be sure to think that Tim had been deliberately destructive.

Hercules picked up the torn skin and examined it. He looked at Tim with a pitying expression. 'I hate to say this, my friend, but you were wrong. This is not a man-eater after all! It's just a skin. See?' Hercules slung the rug on like a cloak. The tiger's jaw rested on his forehead like a hat.

Tim opened his mouth to explain then changed his mind. There was no point. Hercules might be super-strong, but he wasn't super-smart.

'For you.' Hercules took the skin off and wrapped it gently around Tim.

It was hot and heavy and itchy. Tim felt his knees sag from the weight.

'Wear this cloak to school,' Hercules said. 'It shall protect you from arrows.'

'I don't *need* to be protected from arrows.'

'Of course you do. Skinny little lad like you. You need all the help you can get.'

'Get it off me! It's heavy.'

Hercules plucked the rug off Tim as easily as if it were a tea towel. He carried it back into the living room and spread it out on the floor.

'Fine,' said the hero. 'But you know where it is if you ever need it.'

Tim ran into the bathroom and returned with a soft towel. He used it to cover up the tear in the rug.

'I'll fix you later,' he whispered into the tiger's ear. 'Good as new. I promise.'

Straightening, Tim turned to Hercules. 'I have to go to school now.'

'I shall come with you. To keep you safe.'

'You don't need to,' Tim said, backing away. He didn't think he could cope with any more protection. 'School's not far. I always walk by myself.'

Hercules squatted down so he could look Tim in the eye. 'You don't need to be alone any more. You've got me now.'

Tim thought the hero looked sad. 'Um, thanks, but ...' he started to say.

'Being your hero makes me feel better. I miss my little girl. I haven't always been a good father,' he mumbled, his dark eyes haunted. 'That evil Hera tormented me and never gave me peace. She drove me insane. But then I met my new wife and we had Zoe, and I vowed to keep them safe forever.' A giant tear trickled down the hero's cheek.

'I – I'm sorry.' Tim tried to hide his surprise. He didn't know that heroes cried.

Hercules sniffed. 'All I want is to go home and protect my wife and daughter. I can't, I know. But now I've got you to look after.' He smiled at Tim. 'And I'm going to do the job properly,' he added, wiping away the tear.

'Okay.' Tim didn't know what else to say. 'Thanks.'

Looking happier, Hercules followed
Tim out the front door. The garden was
blackened and Tim tried not to look at it.

'Are you sure no one else can see you?'
he asked worriedly. What would his
teacher say? Taking heroes to school was
probably against the rules.

'Sure I'm sure. Look.' Hercules waved
at a mother with a pram. She looked right
through him and kept on walking.

Tim nodded, relieved. As they turned
a corner, Hercules suddenly stiffened.
Tim followed his gaze. An old lady was
walking a dog. The dog was big and
black and strong. It bristled at the sight
of them. Looking straight at Hercules, it
showed its teeth and growled.

'It can see you,' Tim whispered, alarmed. 'Quick, let's cross the road.'

Hercules' eyes narrowed. He locked his fingers together and cracked his knuckles. 'No need to be frightened, Tim Baker. You've got me to protect you now!

STAND BACK,

I don't want you to get hurt.'

7

'I – I don't need to be protected,' Tim
stammered. 'It's much easier to just cross
the road.' He looked at the big dog in alarm.
It continued to stare and growl at them.

Hercules stared and growled back.
'You know, that mutt looks familiar ...'
His voice trailed off as he squinted hard
at the dog.

'How come it can see you when nobody
else can?' Tim kept his voice to a low

whisper so that the old lady wouldn't hear him. He didn't want her to think he was talking to himself.

'Dogs have superpowers too. Their noses can smell the sweat on a flea,' Hercules said. 'And if it's what I think … if I remember rightly … this beast is more powerful than most.'

'B-beast?' Tim didn't like the sound of that. He put a restraining hand on Hercules' arm. 'It's not a–'

'Cerberus!' Hercules roared. 'We meet again!'

The dog barked an angry reply.

'Who …?'

'Cerberus, you hellhound! I shall banish you back to the Underworld, where you belong. What have you done with your other two heads?'

'His what?'

'He has three heads, all with razor-sharp fangs. One bite and you're done for.'

'This dog's only got one head.' Tim felt he should point that out.

'It likes to hide the other two. Don't be fooled. King Eurystheus set me twelve labours to prove my strength. Capturing Cerberus was the final test, which I passed brilliantly of course. I'd know that beast anywhere.' Hercules' gaze never wavered from the dog.

'That was a long time ago.' Sweat broke out on Tim's brow. 'It can't be the same dog.'

'CERBERUS, YOU FIEND!

Lying in wait to exact your revenge. You shall not have it.'

'It's not a fiend, it's a pet,' Tim said, gripping Hercules more tightly. 'Look, it's got an owner.'

Hercules peered at the old lady holding the lead. She was glancing around nervously, clearly wondering what was upsetting her dog. Tim glanced away and tried to act casual, as if it had nothing to do with him.

'Calm down, boy,' she murmured. She looked scared.

'See how Cerberus frightens her? I shall save her. Fear not, old crone, Hercules is here!' He shook off Tim's

hand and strode purposefully towards
the dog.

Frenzied barking filled the air. Lunging
forward, the dog pulled free of its
owner's grasp. It threw itself at Hercules,
growling and snapping.

'Think you're stronger than me?' the
hero snarled. 'I'll teach
you!' With one hand,
he picked the dog
up and raised

it high in the air. The dog paddled its feet
wildly and snapped its jaws.

'ADMIT DEFEAT, VILE HOUND!'

The old lady's hand fluttered to her
mouth. Tim realised how preposterous
this would appear to her. She couldn't see
Hercules, so it must look as though her
dog were floating.

'Put. It. Down.' Tim ordered.

Hercules lowered the dog to the ground.
He briskly wrapped the lead around its
paws. The dog struggled and whimpered,
but it couldn't move. Making soothing
noises, the old lady bustled over to her pet.
She started to unwind the lead, darting

nervous glances at Tim. She must have noticed that her pet had stopped levitating as soon as Tim spoke. The dog licked her hand and wagged its tail. Tim was glad it was all right.

'Let's go,' he said, tugging at Hercules' chiton. He had to get them away from there. 'I can't be late for school.'

'Oh. Right.' Hercules looked at the lady patting the dog. 'The beast has been subdued and the old crone is safe now. All thanks to me.' He puffed out his chest proudly.

■　■　■

Luckily school was only a few streets away. As they approached the gate, Tim turned to Hercules and said, 'This is it, we're here. You can go home now.'

'I shall stay and protect you.'

'No that's okay, I'm fine.'

But Hercules stood his ground and folded his arms as if the matter were settled.

Tim couldn't risk it. Who knew what trouble Hercules would cause at school?

'I don't need protecting!' Tim thought quickly. 'I need help. I need you to go home and sweep. Do you know how to sweep?' He mimed a broom-swishing action.

'Of course I do,' Hercules scoffed. 'I'm the mightiest sweeper in the world. In fact, I can super-sweep. Wait and see.' He spun on his feet and hurried away.

Tim's shoulders sagged with relief. Turning, he trudged across the playground.

'Who were you talking to?' It was his best friend, Ajay, falling into step beside him.

Tim jumped. He hadn't noticed him approaching.

'WHAT? WHEN? NO ONE.'

'At the gate. It looked like you were talking, but there wasn't anyone there. Were you talking to yourself?' Ajay barked with laughter, his soft black eyes sparkling.

'Yes. Yes I was.' Tim nodded vigorously.

Ajay flashed him a suspicious glance. 'What's going on? Tell me.'

Tim was tempted. What was the point of having an exciting secret if he couldn't share it with his best friend? He hesitated for a moment and then the words tumbled out in a rush. 'All right. But only if you promise not to tell anyone.'

'I promise.'

Tim dropped his voice as they approached their classroom. 'I've got a hero.'

'Big deal,' Ajay said, dumping his bag on the floor outside the room. 'Lots of people have heroes. Mine's Harry Potter.'

'No I mean a real one, not a story one. He's in my house.'

'Huh? Whaddya mean?'

In a low voice, Tim told Ajay everything.

Ajay's eyes grew wider and wider and brighter and brighter. When Tim finally stopped talking, Ajay punched him softly on the arm.

'You're joking.'

'It's true,' Tim insisted. 'Hercules said he'd help me with the cleaning but—'

'What's up, Cinderella?' A sneering voice cut off his sentence. Tim whirled around to see Leo sneering at him. His worst enemy was standing right behind them! Tim wondered how much he'd heard.

Too much, as it turned out.

'You need a fairy godmother, not a hero!' Leo brayed. 'Dude, you can't even lie properly.'

'Go away,' Ajay snapped. 'No one's talking to you.'

Leo snickered as he plucked a jelly bean

out of his pocket and popped it into his
mouth. 'Hey, do you want me to punch
Tim too?' he said to Ajay. Leo clenched his
hand into a fist and thrust it near Tim's
face. 'I can punch harder. Here, I'll show
you.' He drew back his meaty arm.

Tim flinched and closed his eyes. He
expected to feel searing pain as his nose

was mashed against his face. Instead, he heard footsteps; the clacking sound of high heels tapping impatiently across the asphalt towards them.

'What are you boys doing here?' It was their teacher's voice. 'The bell's about to ring. Time to line up for assembly. Off you go.' Miss Omiros shooed them away with a flick of her long red fingernails.

'Lucky for you this time, loser,' Leo said, dropping his fist and sticking his face near Tim's. He came so close that Tim could smell his sickly sweet breath.

'Next time, you're gonna need your hero to save you. Pity he's not real.'

The school day passed in misery. Leo teased Tim about Hercules every chance he could. Ajay stood up for Tim, but it was clear he didn't believe him either. By the end of the day Tim was sick of it. He wished he'd kept Hercules a secret.

'Aren't you going to show me your hero?' Leo asked when the home-time bell rang.

Tim gritted his teeth. 'I can't. He's invisible.'

'Right. Invisible, oh yeah I forgot. Still, I wanna see your burnt garden. And the ripped tiger rug.' Leo curled his hands into fists and cracked his knuckles. 'Then I might believe you.'

'I'm busy,' Tim said, turning away.

'Will you be okay?' Ajay asked, taking a halting step towards him. 'I'll walk home with you if you like.'

'Nah, I'll be all right.'

Tim was glad Ajay wanted to help, but couldn't help feeling a little annoyed that his best friend hadn't believed his big secret. In any case, if Leo wanted to get mean, there wasn't much Ajay could do to stop him. Leo was bigger than both of them. It was far better to avoid a face-off, and get home as quickly as possible.

Tim decided not to mention his other worry. He remembered the hero boasting about being able to super-sweep. Tim wondered what that meant. He had a sinking feeling he was about to find out. Without looking back, Tim hurried out of the school gate and down the road. His pulse quickened when he heard Leo lumbering after him.

'OI, CINDERELLA!

Slow down. What's the rush? Bet ya can't wait to show me your secret hero.' Leo snickered unpleasantly.

Tim ignored him. Picking up his pace, he sprinted as fast as his legs would carry him, his school bag thumping against his back. He should be able to outpace the bully. Leo was big, but he was heavy. He lurched rather than walked. Soon Tim was pushing open his front gate. He hurried to the front door.

The door opened and Hercules stepped out. 'Welcome home, my friend! Come in and see—'

'Hey dude! For real? You actually burned your garden?' Leo panted as he approached the house. The bully was faster than he looked. 'Didn't your Mum tell you not to play with matches?'

'Who is this fat worm?' Hercules asked, his eyes narrowing.

'Don't worry about him. Let's go inside.'

Tim tried to dart around Hercules but the hero held him back.

'What does he want?'

'Trouble,' Tim said, pressing his lips together.

'Then he shall have it!' Hercules boomed, his face like thunder.

'Let's just go inside.'

Leo smirked. 'Talking to yourself now?

Man oh man. You're even crazier than I thought.'

'Allow me to chain that worm to a rock,' Hercules said. 'I shall set eagles to peck out his liver and rats to feast on his eyeballs.'

Tim shuddered. 'Please, no. Just, um, show me your super-sweeping.'

Hercules' eyes brightened. 'You want to see?

Right. Follow me.'

But first he took a deep breath
and turned towards Leo. Puffing out
his cheeks, the hero blew a long stream
of air straight at the bully. It made the
leaves rustle in the trees and the dirt
skitter along the ground. Leo staggered
backwards as if he had been pushed by an
invisible hand. He tripped and fell hard, his
teeth snapping together. His face clouded
with fury.

'Ouch! You pushed me! How'd ya
do that?'

Tim didn't answer him. He tugged on Hercules' arm. 'Let's go.'

'If you insist,' Hercules said, still eyeing up Leo, 'but I was enjoying myself.'

Tim slammed the front door and locked it. Feeling better, he walked down the hallway. It was good to have a hero. Leo would think twice about coming back!

Tim started to relax, until he entered the living room. It was completely empty. No sofa, no television, no coffee table. The usually overloaded mantelpiece was bare. With a sinking feeling in the pit of his stomach, Tim darted up the stairs and into the first bedroom – Mum's room. The bed, chest and wardrobe had all vanished. Not a stick of furniture remained. Gasping, he dashed to his own bedroom. It was utterly bare too.

Tim rushed from room to room, eyes bulging. 'Where's all our stuff gone?'

'HAH! I WILL SHOW YOU.'

Tim followed Hercules into the backyard. Spread across the garden were the contents of the entire house. From fence to fence, right down to the creek at the bottom of the garden. Beds, tables, chairs. Books, shoes, cups. All piled high in messy heaps.

'I super-swept. The house has never been cleaner!'

Tim's hands shook. He didn't think he could take much more today.

'You're supposed to sweep out the dirt, not the whole house! Quick, we've got to put everything back before Mum comes home. She'll go nuts!'

'If you insist.' Hercules looked displeased. 'But I think I did a good job.'

Tim and his hero raced around. Huffing and puffing, they put things back as fast as they could, racing to finish before Mum returned.

They almost made it.

■ ■ ■

Mum arrived while Tim was picking the final fork out of the flower bed. Shading her eyes, she stood at the back door and called out. 'What on earth are you doing?'

Tim ran over to her, dirt sprinkling

onto the ground.

'Ah. Err. Hi. You see, Hercules tried to help with the cleaning …'

'*Don't* start that again. I'm not in the mood for stories.' Mum rubbed her eyes and stomped off into the kitchen.

Something had upset her, Tim could tell. Something more serious than grubby cutlery.

Sighing, Mum threw herself into a chair. 'My book's been rejected again. That's the tenth time. Guess I should give up now.'

Tim was stunned. Mum never talked about giving up. 'You can't. You said you'd always keep trying. That one day you'd make it.'

'I've been fooling myself. It's not fair on you, darling. All these dreams of being a writer, they're a waste of time.'

'They're not.'

Mum cupped his chin and smiled. It was a sad smile. 'I have to get real. I'm not going to get published. There's only one way I can make enough money to quit my second job. We'll have to sell the old Greek vase.'

There was a pause. It was long and uncomfortable. It felt like time had slowed down. Tim could hear the clock ticking out the seconds in the hallway.

'Mum. There's something I have to tell you. That vase.' Tim gulped. 'I broke it.'

Mum shook her head, as if she hadn't heard properly. 'What was that, dear?'

'I broke the vase. I'm so sorry. I was cleaning it; the phone rang and ...'

Mum's face went white with shock. She didn't look angry. Just sad.

'I was going to glue it back together,' Tim added, 'and make it good as new.'

'Let me see. We might be able to fix it.' Mum heaved herself out of the chair and followed Tim into the living room.

With shaking hands, Tim pulled the pieces out of the drawer and spread them out in a neat row near the tiger-skin rug. Together they sat on the floor and looked at the broken vase. It was like a giant jigsaw puzzle. Mum's shoulders drooped as she tried to slot a few of the pieces together.

'That's Hercules, fighting a bull. It was one of his twelve labours.' She smiled sadly at the picture. 'Your father bought this for me because he said I was bullheaded.'

Tim gave her a puzzled look. 'Your head doesn't look like a bull's.'

Mum chuckled. 'I'm glad to hear it.'

Tim peered at the drawing. The bull didn't look anything like Mum. Then again, the muscleman didn't look much like Hercules either.

Mum picked up more chunks of vase and looked at the Greek letters despondently. 'I've always wondered what this says. Now I'll never know.'

'Does that mean we can't put it back together?' Tim asked, his fingernails digging into his palms.

'We can, but there's no point. The vase will be worthless. No one will pay good money for something that's been repaired in so many places. Pity.' She sighed.

Tim buried his face in Mum's shoulder. 'Now you'll have to keep working forever.

It's all my fault.'

'Hey, that's okay. Don't cry.'

'I'm not crying,' Tim said, blinking
rapidly. 'I got dust in my eye. I haven't
cleaned up in here yet.'

Mum engulfed Tim in a huge hug.

Tears glistened in her eyes. 'Bad things happen for a reason,' she murmured into his mop of hair. 'Guess this means I have to keep writing. The next story will be better. Someone will like it. You'll see.'

■   ■   ■

Although he didn't get in trouble for breaking the vase, Tim went to bed feeling terrible. He'd glued the vase together, just in case … but Mum was right. It was covered with so many criss-crossing fracture lines that it looked like a spiderweb was wrapped around it.

Nobody would pay for a vase like that.

The next morning Tim awoke to silence. Something was wrong. It took him a moment to realise what it was:

Hercules was not snoring.

Tim leapt out of bed, ran down the stairs and into the living room. Hercules wasn't asleep on the sofa. Tim hoped the hero hadn't decided to do some early morning cleaning. Suddenly, a loud thud came from the kitchen. Fearful of what he might find, Tim inched down the hallway. Another thud. Followed by a burp.

'Very tasty,' Hercules said as Tim walked in. 'What else have you got?' The floor was littered with empty food packets. Cereal, biscuits, cakes. All opened, eaten, and dumped onto the floor.

'Not much, by the look of it,' Tim replied, eyeing up the pantry.

'What's this?' Hercules held up a tin of

peaches. 'The picture on it shows fruit, but when I tried to bite it, it tasted of metal.'

'The fruit's inside,' Tim explained. 'You need a can opener. I'll get it.'

But he didn't need to bother. Before Tim had a chance to move, Hercules squeezed out the tin's contents as if it were a tube of toothpaste.

'Lovely,' he slurped. 'Is there any more?'

'Later. Help me clear this mess before Mum sees it.'

Tim opened the bin to throw out the empty food packets. He froze.

Mum's story was there, covered in crumbs. She had given up! Tim pulled the pages out and spread them neatly on the kitchen table. They weren't rubbish. Maybe if Mum saw that Tim had saved them, she'd start working on the story again.

'You'd better stay at school with me today,' Tim said as they cleared up. He couldn't risk leaving Hercules home alone again. 'But you have to behave. Can you do that?'

'Me? Of course I can. Why, I'll super-behave! You'll see.'

Tim kept his fingers crossed all the way to school. Part of him was worried that Hercules might cause trouble. Another part was glad to have the hero with him, in case Leo wanted revenge for being knocked to the ground.

'Sit in the playground and wait for me,' Tim told Hercules as they walked through the gate. He pointed to a long metal bench outside his classroom door. 'Don't move from here.'

'Hey! Talking to invisible heroes again? Man oh man, you need someone to fix you up.' Leo seemed to appear out of nowhere. He looked around uncertainly, then bumped Tim hard with his bag, sending him sprawling on his hands and knees. 'That's for knocking me over yesterday,' he hissed. 'I don't know how you did it, but …' Still glancing left and right, Leo turned and strode away.

Hercules helped Tim to his feet. He dusted him down.

'Are you hurt? I shall swat that worm like the insect he is,' the hero growled.

'I'd rather forget it.'

'Why do you let him treat you like that?' Hercules asked, bending down and peering into Tim's face.

Tim shrugged miserably. His knees stung and bits of gravel clung to his palms.

'Tim Baker, you have to stand up for yourself.'

'How?'

'WRESTLE HIM.

Throw him to the floor and tie him up with stout ropes. That's what I did with the wild pig of Erymanthus. It should work, that boy looks like a pig.'

'I – I don't think that's a good idea.'

Tim adjusted his collar, which had twisted sideways as he fell. 'He's bigger than me.'

The hero snorted. 'It matters not. I have defeated monsters taller than trees, mightier than mountains. It's easy. I shall show you how.'

Just then, the morning bell rang. All the children started to dash towards the assembly area. 'Don't do anything!' Tim begged. 'I've got to line up with the others. Just sit on the bench and don't move. Please.'

'All right, I will wait,' Hercules agreed. 'But remember what I said. Say the word, and the bully shall be beaten.'

Hercules strode towards the bench and sat down. His legs were so long that his knees pressed up against his chest. The bench sagged under his weight, bending at the middle.

All morning, Tim darted glances through the open classroom door. Sure enough, Hercules stayed on the seat. He twiddled his thumbs. He chewed his nails. But he did not move. Tim started to relax. Maybe everything would be all right. Leo was ignoring him and Hercules was behaving.

Two hours passed and it was nearly break time.

That was when the trouble began.

From the corner of his eye, Tim saw
something move. He snapped his head
around. Hercules had left the bench. He
had come up to the classroom. Right
outside, where all the school bags were
lined up.

'Food, I need food,' Hercules mumbled.

'Psst,' Tim hissed from the corner of his
mouth. 'Go away!'

Either Hercules couldn't hear, or he

ignored Tim's warning. The hero plunged his hand into someone's bag. Grinning, he pulled out an apple. It was gone in one gulp. Hercules stuck his hand in another bag, then another. Each time he found more food and swallowed it whole.

'No!' Tim shouted, forgetting to be quiet.

'Is there a problem?' Miss Omiros asked, her heels tapping across the floor.

Tim opened and closed his mouth. Just as he was trying to work out what to say, the bell rang for break.

'I'll talk to you later, Tim,' the teacher said. 'You may all get your morning snacks and go outside.'

Chattering happily, the children ran over to their bags.

'What was that about?' Ajay asked as he rummaged for his break-time snack. 'Hercules causing trouble again?'

'Yes,' Tim said, even though he knew that Ajay was only teasing.

Tim watched as one by one the children went to Miss Omiros to complain that someone had taken their food.

'I bet it was Tim,' Leo told her, his lip curling. 'He's so poor, he has to steal to eat.'

'That's enough, Leo,' Miss Omiros said sharply. 'Go outside.'

Tim turned to go too, but the teacher stopped him.

'Tim, I want to see your bag.'

'You can't believe Leo!' Ajay piped up. 'He's just being mean.'

'I know. But I noticed Tim was the only one not to look in his bag. Why not?'

Tim couldn't tell the teacher the real reason. Hercules had eaten all of his food on the way to school, so he knew there'd be nothing to eat.

'I – I ...' Tim shifted his weight from

one foot to the other.

'Who were you talking to before?'

'Nobody. I was – uh – thinking out loud.' Tim looked across the playground warily. After gobbling everyone's lunches, Hercules had disappeared. Tim had to find him before he managed to eat all the food in the school.

'Show me your bag. I want to look inside.'

Tim hurriedly opened his bag for Miss Omiros.

There was no food in it.

'All right,' the teacher said, eyes narrowing. 'You may go play. But I'll be watching you.'

Tim didn't have time to worry about

that. He had to find Hercules. Heart pounding, he ran across the playground. He thought he knew where Hercules would be.

In the canteen.

He was right. Behind the counter, next to the dinner ladies, was his hero. Unseen by everyone except Tim, Hercules picked his way through a jar of breadsticks. Munching and crunching and chomping.

Barging to the front of the queue, Tim shouted, 'No, don't eat that!'

Everyone turned and stared. Tim knew he looked crazy, but he had no choice. He had to get Hercules out of there.

'Go to the end of the line,' one of the dinner ladies said, glaring at him. She was standing right next to the ancient hero.

'Put down that muffin!' Tim ordered, glaring at Hercules. 'And go home.'

The plump woman sucked in her breath. 'Who do you think you're talking to, young man?'

'I can't say,' Tim said. Then he added to

Hercules, 'You've had more than enough already. You'll get fat.'

'How dare you?' the woman said shrilly, holding in her stomach.

Hercules licked his lips as he picked up a sandwich. 'All right, my friend. I'll go as soon as I finish this.'

Tim's head drooped. He felt relieved. But not for long.

A hand fell on his shoulder. It was Miss Omiros. 'Tim Baker. You're coming to see the principal. Right now.'

■ ■ ■

'Not fair,' Tim mumbled on his way home. Lunchtime detention. He hadn't called the canteen lady fat! He'd been talking to Hercules.

After much thought, Tim had decided to tell the principal the truth. An invisible hero was on the loose. Tim had been trying to stop him. The principal had pressed her lips together in a long, thin line. She didn't believe Tim. No one ever did. From now on, he would keep Hercules a dead secret … from everybody.

Faint with hunger from a day without food, Tim entered the kitchen, hoping he could find something to eat. What he saw made him wish he had after-school detention, too.

Flour was strewn all over the floor. Cracked eggs were splattered on the tiles. Mixing bowls and frying pans sat in rivers of butter. Tim leapt over a milk puddle.

'What happened?' he yelped.

'Pancakes,' Hercules replied, brushing crumbs off his chiton. 'I was feeling peckish. Do you like pancakes? I used to make them for my daughter.'

'How will I ever clean it?' Tim felt like tearing out his hair.

'Worry not, I've fixed bigger messes than this. One of my labours was to clean the Augean Stables. You wouldn't believe how dirty they were. The smell! Piles of horse dung this high.' Hercules held his hand up to his forehead. 'And I only had one day to do it.'

'Did you manage?' Tim's voice shook.

'Of course I did. Sit down. I shall show you how.'

11

Tim paced nervously as Hercules marched out through the back door. He was doubtful, but what choice did he have? There was no way he could clean all that mess by himself. Soon a scraping, digging sound came from outside. It started at the back door, and moved gradually further away. Right down to the creek that flowed through the bottom of the garden.

Suddenly, the digging was replaced by a

gurgling sound. Like running water.

With a loud *WHOOSH!* a torrent
of creek water sped into the kitchen. It
covered the floor. It soaked Tim's ankles.
It lapped against the cupboard doors.
Within seconds the water was waist-deep.
It churned through the room, swirling the
flour and eggs into a sticky underwater
cyclone.

'This is how I cleaned the stables!'
Hercules shouted over the noise.

'Aargh! A flood, a flood!'

'Pretty smart, eh?'

Tim didn't answer. The water was
creeping up his chest. Sodden leaves from

the creek clung to his shirt and trousers. He scrambled up onto the kitchen table and gaped at the swilling waters below. Tim was a strong swimmer, but hoped it wouldn't come to that.

'Don't worry, my friend. It's under control.'

Hercules thrust his big hands into the water and pushed. The water bubbled and seethed. Then it rushed outside. Hercules forced it all the way back to the creek. The floor was sopping wet … but sparkling clean. All traces of dirt and debris had been washed away.

Dripping, Tim jumped to the floor. He rushed to the back door and watched the creek water recede to its proper place.

'See?' Hercules said, wiping his hands on a dry bit of chiton. 'All done. Nothing to worry about.'

Except for one thing. Tim's face turned white when he saw it.

Mum's story had been swept off the kitchen table by the flood waters! Washed up in a corner, the pages were soaked right through. Shrieking, Tim

tried to scoop it up. It was so soggy it
fell apart in his hands.

HER STORY WAS RUINED!

Tim attempted to wring the water out
but that just made the problem worse.

He was still trying to stick the torn
pages together when Mum came home.
They were damp and the sticky tape kept
peeling off.

'What happened?' Mum asked,
splashing across the kitchen tiles. 'How
did you get so wet? Why's there water on
the floor?'

'Your story.' Tim's voice trembled as he
held up the sodden pages. 'It's wrecked.
I'm sorry.'

'Never mind about that. It's only a copy. The manuscript's still on the computer.' Mum waved the paper away as she opened a cupboard and looked under the sink. 'Maybe a water pipe burst. Hmm. Doesn't look like it. Strange.'

Tim didn't know what to say. Hercules sat in a kitchen chair and watched with a smile on his face.

Mum looked at Tim, eyebrows lowered. 'Timothy. *Where* did all this water come from? I want the truth.'

The truth? Last time he'd told the truth, he'd got detention. Besides, Mum would say he was making things up again. He turned away.

'You won't believe me.'

Mum groaned. She splashed over to
Tim and put an arm around his shoulders.
'I'll try,' she said. 'You can always talk to
me. I won't get angry. Promise.'

Tim looked up at his mum. She looked
back. Tim took a deep breath, as if he
were about to dive into a swimming pool.

He would take a chance. He would try sharing his secret, one last time.

'I think you should sit down.'

He told Mum everything. Right from the beginning. He told her about Hercules being trapped in the vase, and how he escaped when it broke. Tim told her about the weeding. About the tiger-skin rug. About the pancakes and the creek water.

Mum didn't interrupt. She sat quietly with her hands folded in her lap. Her eyes grew bigger and brighter. When Tim finished, he looked at her nervously. Did she believe him?

'Brilliant,' she said. 'What a great idea!'

Beaming, she jumped to her feet. She grabbed a notebook and pen, scribbled and muttered, 'He thought the dog was Cerberus!' She chuckled. 'Right. I've got to write this now, before I forget it.' Mum bustled off to her bedroom, where she kept her computer. She looked excited, the way she always did when she started a new story.

A huge weight lifted from Tim's shoulders. Mum hadn't laughed at him. She hadn't got angry. He wasn't too sure she believed him, but she looked happy. Tim didn't feel so bad about breaking the vase now.

Which reminded him ... he'd been meaning to show Hercules something. This was as good a time as any.

'Hey, Hercules. Come and look at this.'

Tim squelched his way into the living room, trying not to drip onto the tiger-skin rug. He grabbed the glued-together vase and flashed it at the hero. 'See this muscleman? It's meant to be you.'

Hercules peered over Tim's shoulder and grunted. 'Me? Humph! In real life, I am much stronger.' He flexed his muscles to demonstrate. 'At least it shows I'm winning the fight. I beat that bullheaded bull easily.'

'Is that what this says? How you beat the bully?' Tim turned the vase carefully, showing Hercules the lines of writing on the back.

The hero let out a loud gasp. 'Can – can you give it to me?'

'Sure. Why?'

'The writing. I can read it! It says … it says …' Hercules fell silent. His lips moved as he read the ancient words. It took a long time. He clenched and unclenched his fists.

Finally Hercules looked up, his face white with shock.

'My friend. You will never believe what it says.'

12

'Tell me. What does it say?' Tim asked, staring at the writing on the vase.

The hero's lips trembled. 'It says there's a way to send me home. Back to my wife and daughter. Thank the gods; I've missed them so much!'

Tim couldn't help grinning. 'How? How do we do it?'

'We have to do what the vase says. I haven't got to that bit yet … but I, Hercules, shall do whatever it takes. Do I need to wrestle a bull? Easy! Do I need to hold up the sky? Simple!'

'Well, what does it say?' Tim asked, wishing he could read it himself; it would be quicker.

Hercules peered at the jagged writing, his brow furrowing with the effort. It took a long time, but Tim kept quiet. When Hercules finally finished, his eyelids drooped and his shoulders slumped. He looked at Tim, his face a mask of misery.

'What's wrong?' Tim asked. Surely his hero could do anything!

'It is too hard. I thought it might be hero work, but it's not. It's … a puzzle.'

Startled, Tim jumped. He loved puzzles.

'You probably haven't noticed, but I'm not very smart. Surprising I know. But now I'll never go home.' Hercules started to cry. Big fat tears trickled down his cheeks. They splashed onto the floor.

'I'm good at puzzles,' Tim said hastily. He had to stop Hercules crying before the house was flooded again.

'You are?' A look of hope flashed across the hero's face. 'Can you help me go home, Tim Baker?'

Tim didn't want Hercules to go. Despite the trouble he'd caused, Tim liked him. Besides, it was kind of cool to know a hero, even if he did have to keep it a secret from most people. But Hercules looked so sad, and he missed his family so much …

'I'm sure I can,' Tim replied firmly. 'What sort of puzzle is it?'

Hercules sniffed. 'I have to solve a riddle. A riddle! How ridiculous!

Why can't it say hold back the ocean, something simple like that?'

'Read it out.'

'Hang on, I have to find it again.' Hercules ran a finger down the vase. 'Here we go. It says:

> *If you have me, you want to share me.*
> *If you share me, I won't exist.*
> *What am I?'*

Mouth hanging open, Tim stared at Hercules.

'What's the answer?' Hercules asked eagerly. 'Speak it, so I may go home.'

'I'm sorry,' Tim had to say. 'I've no idea.'

'Guess,' Hercules urged. 'You said you were good at puzzles.'

Gazing into the distance, Tim rubbed his chin. 'Hmm. What do you want to share, but if you do it stops existing?'

'That's easy,' Hercules said, holding his stomach. 'I'm not so dumb after all. Food! If you share food, it no longer exists. Because it gets eaten.'

Tim frowned. He wasn't too sure.

'Go on, try that. You have to be the one to say the answer,' Hercules explained, 'because you freed me.'

Tim shrugged. It was worth a try. 'Okay. Food.'

They waited. Nothing happened. Hercules was still there.

'It's wrong, it's wrong,' the hero groaned.

'What do I want to share?' Tim asked

himself. 'Toys? Games? No, they'll exist
even if I share them. Hmm.'

'How about housework?' Hercules
suggested. 'When you share it, it gets
done faster.'

'That might work!
Let's try: housework.'
Again, nothing
happened. Hercules
kicked a chair glumly.
It snapped in half.

'Don't worry,' Tim said, eyeing the broken chair. 'We'll work it out. It just takes time. Hey, is that the answer? Time?' He waited a few seconds. 'Oh. Guess not.'

'This won't work. I'll never go home.' Hercules stamped his foot impatiently. The floor shook and the windows rattled.

'Wait, there might be a clue on the vase. What else does it say?'

The hero's eyes shifted left and right. 'Nothing.'

'But – but it must say more,' Tim protested. 'Look at all those sentences! You've only read a few lines.'

'They … say nothing.' Hercules didn't sound very convincing.

Tim wondered what the hero was trying to hide – and why. 'Well, who wrote the riddle?' he asked. 'Does it say that, at least?'

'Yes.' Hercules lowered himself to the floor as if exhausted. He mopped his brow. 'These are the words of my father, the mighty Zeus, King of the Olympians.'

Tim nodded, waiting for more.

'My father wants me to be able to go home – but only if I can prove myself worthy. Zeus was never happy with my school reports. He used to chain me to a cliff face until I had finished my homework. But hah!' For a moment Hercules looked his old self again.

'No chains could hold me! I snapped them like fish bones and escaped.' Then his eyes drooped again. 'Maybe that was a mistake.'

'That's okay.' Tim leant down and patted the hero awkwardly on the shoulder. 'We'll work it out together.'

Tim tried different answers all evening. None of them worked. No matter how many times he tried, he couldn't guess the answer to the riddle.

The next morning, Hercules was lying on the sofa with his hands over his face.

'Any ideas?' he asked as Tim entered the room.

'Not yet, but I'm still trying. Do you want some breakfast?'

Hercules sighed. 'No thanks. I'm not hungry.'

Tim's eyebrows shot up. 'Not hungry? You?' Tim was worried. Hercules was always hungry. 'Are you coming to school with me today?'

'I'll stay here if you don't mind. I won't clean. I won't cook. I just want to sit.'

Tim didn't want to leave Hercules alone when he looked so sad. He had no choice though. He had to go to school.

'Don't worry. I'll keep working on the puzzle,' Tim promised. 'I know I can do it.' And he crossed his fingers for luck.

Tim headed towards the front door, then paused. He was sure there was more written on the vase than Hercules was letting on. What if it could help him solve the riddle? Tim didn't know whether the hero had trouble reading – or whether it said something he didn't want Tim to know.

But maybe there was a way to find out. Miss Omiros. His teacher was Greek –

she'd mentioned it in class one day.

Tim tiptoed back into the living room. He didn't want Hercules to see what he was about to do and ask awkward questions. He needn't have worried. Hercules was lying on the sofa with his hand over his eyes. Loud snoring filled the room. The hero had gone back to sleep.

Grabbing the vase by its handles, Tim hefted it off the mantelpiece. He left the house as quietly as he could. Once outside, Tim slung his school bag on his back and cradled the vase in his arms. It was big and slippery. Tim had to be very careful; it wouldn't survive another fall. If the vase broke, Hercules might be stranded forever, even if they did manage to solve the riddle. No magic vase, no magic. It stood to reason.

'What're you doing with that?' Ajay asked as Tim trudged across the playground. He hurried over to help. They took a handle each and carried it between them.

'Thanks.' Tim rolled his aching shoulders with relief. 'I'm taking it to Miss Omiros. See if she can read it.'

'How come?'

They were interrupted before Tim could answer.

'OI, CINDERELLA!

What's that ya got?' Leo strode towards them, popping jelly beans into his mouth as he walked.

'None of your business,' Tim snapped, not slowing his pace. 'C'mon Ajay, ignore him.'

'It's not show-and-tell today. Whaddya bring that ugly thing for?'

Tim pressed his lips together and kept walking. He didn't look back. With his free hand, he knocked on the staffroom door. Miss Omiros opened it, a mug of coffee in her hand.

'Miss,' Tim panted, hoisting the vase up higher. 'Can I show you something?'

The teacher let out a low whistle. 'Oh my, an amphora.' She put her mug down before plucking the vase delicately from Tim and Ajay's hands. 'The Ancient Greeks used them to store wine and oil, did you know that?'

Tim shrugged. He knew for a fact they also used them to store heroes, but decided not to mention that.

'Do you know how old it is?' the teacher asked.

'Dunno exactly. Very old. It broke, though, and I had to glue it back together. Can you read what it says?' Tim showed her the writing on the back. 'Mum said it's Greek.'

Frowning, Miss Omiros ran her long red nails over the letters. Tim held his breath. What would it say? Finally, after what felt like ages, the teacher shook her head. 'No, I'm sorry. It's in Ancient Greek. I only know Modern. Some of the words are familiar, but not enough. I've no idea, sorry.'

'Do you know anyone who might?' Tim dared to hope, but Miss Omiros shook her head.

Tim's heart sank. His plan had failed. He was no further forward. The riddle was still unsolved.

He left the vase in the staffroom for safekeeping, then went to class. He hoped Hercules wouldn't notice the vase was missing and come to school to investigate. There was no sign of the hero all day, however. In a way that was worse. Tim hoped Hercules wasn't feeling too upset.

■　■　■

After the home-time bell rang, Tim went to the staffroom to collect the vase. He went alone. Ajay had cricket practice straight after school and couldn't help. Tim gripped the vase with both arms and headed for home. It seemed to grow heavier with each step. Sweat dripped off his face and he had to stop to rest several times. It was like carrying a large, fat baby in his arms; a grouchy, slippery baby that kept trying to slide from his grip.

'Nearly there. I can do it,' Tim muttered as he turned the corner into his street.

Then he froze.

Waiting in front of his house, swinging on the gate, was Leo. The rusty hinges creaked in protest, setting a neighbour's dog barking. Tim had thought Leo wouldn't dare turn up again, not after being flattened by Hercules last time. What did the bully want?

'Shouldn't you be at home?' Tim asked, trying to play it cool. 'Your parents'll be worried.'

To Tim's surprise, Leo's face flushed

bright red.

'Don't talk about my parents!' He kicked the gate with a scuffed shoe. 'Just shut your face.'

'All right,' Tim said. He had no idea what *that* was about. He tried to edge past the bully. 'Whatever. I've got to go in now.'

'Not until you show me what you've got,' Leo said, his voice fierce.

Tim tightened his grip. 'It's just an old vase. Nothing special.'

'Yeah? Then give it to me.' Leo jerked forward and snatched the vase out of Tim's arms.

'Hey, give it back!'

'Not until you tell me what you did

before. You knocked me down without touching me. How'd ya do it?'

'I didn't.' Tim lunged for the vase but missed. 'It … it was the wind.'

'Tell me or I'm gonna drop it.' Leo lifted the vase up high, too high for Tim to reach.

'All right.' Tim's mouth felt dry. He had to say something. He couldn't let Leo destroy Hercules' only chance to go home. 'I didn't do anything. It … it was my hero.'

Leo rolled his eyes. 'Not that hero stuff again. Prove it! Go on. If he's real, I want to see him.'

Leo tossed the vase into the air. Tim's breath jammed in his throat. He didn't exhale again until Leo caught it. 'Put it down, please.'

'Call your hero, Cinderella, or I'll drop it.'

Tim had no choice. He darted past Leo and unlocked the front door.

'HERCULES!'

he shouted down the hallway. 'Hercules, come quickly! I need help.'

Tim and Leo stood breathing heavily, eyes fixed on the doorway. Watching. Waiting.

Nothing happened.

Hercules did not come.

'Pah, I knew it!' Leo spat when Hercules didn't appear. 'You're such a liar. There's no hero. You made it up to sound cool.'

'No I didn't–' Tim stopped when Leo drew his arms back, his grip on the vase loosening.

'I'm gonna smash it. There's no such thing as heroes, Cinderella.'

Tim's mind raced. He had to think of something. For some reason, Hercules wasn't answering his call. It was up to Tim to stop Leo. Like the bull on the vase, the bully was too big to wrestle, but ...

Tim's thoughts flew back to the very first time he had met Hercules. He remembered how surprised he'd been to learn that Hera had sent snakes to kill the infant demigod. It gave him an idea.

'Then watch out for the snake!' Tim cried, throwing up his hands.

Leo's arms paused in mid-air. 'What snake?' A note of uncertainty entered his voice.

'In the vase,' Tim said, struggling to keep his face straight. 'I keep my snake there. I took it to school to show Miss, to see if I can bring it for pet day.'

'There's no snake.' Leo lowered the vase, holding it as far from his chest as possible. His hands shook slightly.

'Yeah there is. His name is Hercules. After the Ancient Greek hero.'

Leo crinkled his nose. 'Is that what all this hero stuff's been about? A stupid snake?'

'Yes.' Tim nodded, letting Leo believe the lie. 'Why, did you think I meant a real hero?' Tim snorted and shook his head.

'But I heard you tell Ajay—'

Tim didn't let Leo finish his sentence. 'Miss said I can't bring the snake for pet day because it's too dangerous. That's why they had to keep it in the staffroom.'

'Too dangerous?' Leo's hands shook harder.

'It's an adder, very venomous. I didn't know that when I trapped it. But I'm not worried. Hercules likes me.' Tim paused and glanced pointedly at the vase. 'I don't think he'll like you, though.'

'You're making it up,' Leo said, his face rigid with fear.

'Oh yeah? Stick your hand in and see.'

'You're weird, ya know that? You can keep your stupid snake.' Leo put the vase carefully on the ground and backed away.

'Come near me again, and I'll set my hero on you!' Tim lunged towards Leo.

'GARR!'

Leo turned and fled.

'See if I care. You're still a loser. I'll fix you up later!' he shouted as he ran, his cheeks wobbling with the effort.

Tim wiped the sweat off his brow and took a deep breath. It had been a close call, but he'd made it.

When his heart went back to normal, he picked up the vase and carried it inside.

■ ■ ■

Hercules was still lying on the sofa, his eyes closed. Tim eased the vase back onto the mantelpiece. He cleared his throat.

'No luck, then,' Hercules said, opening one eye. 'You could not solve the cursed riddle. I can tell, because I'm still here.'

Tim shook his head. Thanks to Leo, he'd almost forgotten about the riddle. 'You?'

'No. Guess we shall have to give up.' He sighed gustily.

'Don't say that, we'll–' Tim stopped. Someone had opened the front door and was walking down the hallway. It was way too early for Mum to come home from work. Had something bad happened?

'Hi darling.' Mum breezed into the living room. A big smile lit up her face. 'Guess what? I'm not going to my second job today. I've taken the day off!'

'Did she get fired?' Hercules moaned. 'This is a bad day for everyone.'

Tim flapped his hand at him to be quiet. He knew it wasn't that. Mum looked too happy.

'I've been to see a publisher. They loved the idea for my new story. They want to publish it!'

'YAY!'

Tim threw himself into her arms. In that instant, he forgot all about Leo. Mum might be able to leave her second job!

'Does that mean you'll always come home early?'

'Eventually. Maybe. It'll take a while, mind you, but one day it might happen. Then you won't have to do all the housework any more.'

Tim grinned. That was good, but having Mum home was better.

'All thanks to you.' Mum gave Tim a loud kiss on the cheek. Her lipstick left a sticky patch. Tim wriggled uncomfortably. 'My story's called *Hercules the Housekeeper*,' Mum continued, licking her thumb and wiping off the red mark from Tim's face. 'He's strong but makes mistakes. He gets into all sorts of trouble. You gave me the idea when you shared your wonderful secret with me.'

Hercules groaned from the sofa, but Tim didn't turn his head to look. He stared at his Mum. 'Does that mean you believed me? You know I didn't make him up?'

Mum didn't answer. Instead she said, 'How about we get takeaway to celebrate? Today's too special for cheese on toast.'

'Yeah! Can we have chicken and chips?' Tim picked something he knew Hercules would like. He wanted to share his happiness with his friend. Maybe the food would help cheer him up.

'You bet,' Mum said, patting Tim's cheek. 'I'll go get it. Want to come with me?'

Suddenly Tim froze. Something

Mum said had given him a clue. Finally, everything clicked into place. He knew the answer to the puzzle!

'Um, no. That's okay. I'll stay here.'

'Sure? All right. Won't be long.'

Tim waited impatiently for Mum to go. As soon as he heard the front door click shut, he darted to the sofa and whispered in Hercules' ear.

Delighted, the hero leapt to his feet.

'Yes, that sounds right. It must be it.' Hercules engulfed Tim in a giant hug. Tim felt his ribs creak under the pressure. 'I don't know how to thank you, Tim Baker.'

'You don't need to thank me,' Tim gasped, pulling away and rubbing at his sides. 'You helped me too. I couldn't get all three wishes but I got one ...'

Hercules looked puzzled, then his face broke into a giant grin. 'You beat the bully?'

'Yep. I did.' Tim nodded.

'Did you do what I told you?

Did you tie him up with ropes? Chain him to a boulder? Pick him up and hurl him into the deepest pits of the Underworld?'

'Nope, nothing like that.' Tim's eyes glowed. 'Something better: I tricked him.'

Hercules raised his eyebrows. 'With your brain? You are clever indeed. Puzzle solver and bully beater!' He reached over and ruffled Tim's hair, making it stand up in wild tufts. 'And now, thanks to you, I can see my wife and daughter again. Agatha, Zoe, I am coming home!' Tears filled Hercules' eyes.

Tim didn't want his hero to leave, but he knew he had to let him go. 'Are you ready?' Tim whispered, smoothing his hair back down. 'Shall we do it now?'

'Yes. Now.' Hercules pulled himself to

his full height. 'I'll say the riddle and you answer it. Here we go:

> *If you have me, you want to share me.*
> *If you share me, I won't exist.*
> *What am I?'*

Tim smiled. He nodded once, twice. Then he spoke.

'A secret.'

Sparkles of golden light shone around the hero. 'It's working. I can feel it. Goodbye, Tim Baker. I will always remember you, my clever friend!'

Hercules waved as the sparkles grew bigger and brighter, forming a thick shimmering mist.

Then it vanished, along with the hero. Tim was alone in the room.

But not for long.

Mum would be back soon with a celebration feast.

15

That night, Tim awoke to an unfamiliar noise. Something was moving about in the darkness. Groggy with sleep, he opened his eyes. Tim always slept with his bedroom door open. The house was pitch black: the only light was the soft grey square of his bedroom window.

His first thought was that Hercules must be hunting for a midnight snack. It was the wrong sort of sound, however.

This was stealthy. Sneaky. A soft scraping, a few seconds of silence, then a slither. Hercules wouldn't be so quiet. Hercules would stomp around the kitchen noisily, not creep along the hallway like an oversized snake.

Then Tim remembered. The hero had gone home. It couldn't be him.

Maybe it was Mum moving about. But wouldn't she turn on the light?

Tim climbed out of bed.

As quietly as he could, he stepped out onto the landing. The sound was coming from downstairs. He darted into Mum's room. He could see her dark outline in bed.

'Mum,' he whispered, tugging at the blankets. 'Wake up.'

'Mmmm … wha …' Mum mumbled.

'There's someone in the house.'

'Thass nice … say hi …' she rolled over to face the wall.

'Mum,' Tim spoke more urgently. The sound of her soft snoring filled the room.

Another bump, then a crash. Tim jumped. He wished Hercules was still there. Heart pounding, Tim shut his mother's door. He inched down the staircase. He could hear voices coming from the living room. A woman's and a man's.

INTRUDERS!

They spoke softly. Tim had to creep closer to hear what they were saying.

'I can't see it anywhere, Your Majesty.'

'It's here. I know it is,' the woman hissed. 'Look harder!'

'Yes, Your Majesty.' A bump, followed by a curse. 'I'm trying, but it's too dark.'

The woman let out an irritated sigh, then Tim heard the sound of fingers clicking. The room flooded with dazzling light. Keeping to the shadows, he peered through the doorway. It took his eyes a moment to adjust. He rubbed them, wondering if he was seeing things.

Standing in the middle of the room were two shimmering figures. A tall, thin woman with jet-black hair and very pale skin. She wore a long, ivory-coloured gown. On her head was a dainty crown with a transparent veil trailing down the back. Next to her was a young man in a short white chiton. His cap and sandals had feathery wings attached to them. They fluttered as he stumbled around the room.

'Find it. Find it now,' the woman commanded.

'Yes, Your Majesty.' The young man bumped into a pot plant, knocking it sideways. It screeched as it skidded across the floorboards.

'Careful, you clumsy oaf! Do you wish to awaken the household?'

'Yes, Your Majesty. I mean no, Your Majesty.' The young man ducked and bowed. 'Forgive me, Queen Hera.'

Tim jumped as he recognised the name. This was the evil woman who had trapped Hercules in the vase! What was she doing here?

'Find what I seek. Retrieve my vase at once, Hermes, or your punishment shall be severe.'

She wanted the vase back! Tim's breath caught in his throat.

'It's hard to find anything in this mess,' the man called Hermes complained, nudging a cushion aside with his foot.

'No excuses!' Hera hissed. 'This *is* the home of Tim Baker, is it not?'

'It is, Your Majesty.' As if gathering courage, Hermes shook himself before continuing. 'Maybe he read the writing on the vase, my Queen. Maybe he figured out what it can do.'

'Nonsense,' Hera snapped. 'He would not have sufficient wit.'

'Hercules said the boy is smart.'

Hera snorted. 'That idiot! A slug is smart compared to Hercules.' Hera's pale blue eyes were like chips of ice. 'Now the buffoon walks around town as if he owns the place. I won't have it! I shall trap him again, this time forever. But first – find my vase.'

'Didn't Hercules say it was broken? They might have thrown it out.'

'They did not! It is here. I can feel its presence. They must have repaired it.' Hera swayed like a snake as she strode around the room. 'Where is it? Where?!'

'Maybe in here, Your Majesty,' Hermes said, peering inside the fireplace.

Not looking where he was going,

he stumbled over the tiger-skin rug.
'Yah!' Arms spinning wildly, he jerked
backwards, knocking the queen goddess
over. She sprawled on the ground in
an undignified heap, her crown pushed
sideways.

'YOU IDIOT!'

Hera cursed, straightening her veil. 'Can't
you see where you're going? No – do not
touch me.' She ignored the trembling hand
Hermes extended. She rose to her feet in
one fluid motion. 'Look at what you've
done.' Hera held out her index finger and
shook it menacingly.

Tim squinted, trying to see what she
was talking about.

'You chipped my nail, Hermes. Now I'll have to go home and file it.'

Hermes shrank backwards. 'I'm so sorry, Your Majesty. Forgive me.'

'You fool. Take me home then return at once. Find the vase. Do not dare to show your face until you succeed.' Hera held out her hand regally. Hermes, bowing, took her hand and they shot up to the ceiling before vanishing. Tim gaped, stunned. Seconds later, Hermes reappeared, this time on his own.

The young man stumbled around the room, wings flapping frantically as he searched. Tim eyed the vase on the mantelpiece. He had to stop Hermes taking it. But how?

'Ah.' Hermes spotted the vase. His eyes glittered.

'Garr!' With an ear-piercing shout, Tim flung himself into the room. He swept past Hermes, who spun around in bewilderment. Moving quickly, Tim lunged for the vase. He clasped it in his arms and held on tight.

'Give it to me, boy.' Hermes' voice was sharp.

'NO.'

'You must.'

Tim pressed his lips into a thin, hard line.

'If you don't, Hera will punish you. She'll come back and snare you.' Head

drooping, Hermes added in a softer voice,
'She'll punish me, too.'

Tim lifted the vase high into the air.
'Come closer and I'll smash it,' he warned,
silently thanking Leo for giving him
the idea.

The last thing Tim wanted was to break the vase. He wanted to keep it as a reminder of his hero, but the bluff might just work.

Hermes' chin wobbled. 'I'll tell the queen on you. She'll be well angry. You won't get away with this, Tim Baker.' The wings on his cap and sandals flapped more vigorously. The young man floated up to the ceiling, where he bobbed up and down. 'You'll see!' And then he vanished.

Shaking, Tim cradled the vase and took it into his bedroom. From now on, he would have to keep a very close eye on it. For Hercules' sake …

… and for his own.

Look out for Tim's next adventure...

...COMING SOON.

HOPELESS HEROES

HERA'S TERRIBLE TRAP!

1

Tim Baker wrapped his scarf around his neck. It was unusually cold for May. The clouds were heavy with rain despite the fine weather forecast. As if defying the television newsreader, a splatter of rain plonked firmly onto Tim's forehead and slithered down his nose.

He shuddered.

There were plenty of other things he'd rather be doing on a soggy Sunday

morning. Like playing computer games
in his cosy living room. Or chatting with
his best friend, Ajay. Or even – yep – *even*
finishing off his maths homework. But no.
He couldn't do any of those things. Tim
fished a damp tissue out of his pocket and
blew his nose glumly.

An outdoor garden centre! Of all things! Row after row of nothing but leaves, stems and petals. And a whole bunch of adults in mackintoshes nodding and making *ooh* and *ah* sounds, as if they'd never seen a plant before. Really, didn't they have anything better to do with their time?

Not that there was anything amazing waiting for him at home, Tim realised, a lump forming in his throat. Not since his good friend Hercules had left.

Tim's adventures had started when he accidentally broke an Ancient Greek vase his mother owned. Incredibly, an enormous figure had erupted out through the cracks. At first Tim thought he'd released a genie. Instead it turned out to be the hero Hercules. Half human, half god, Hercules was the son of a mortal woman and Zeus, king of the Olympian gods. Not what you normally find in an ornament, but since then Tim had learnt to expect the unexpected.

Hercules had been trapped in the vase thousands of years ago by Hera, Zeus' wife. The queen goddess was jealous of Hercules' beautiful mother. From the moment the demigod was born, Hera had decided to hate and resent him. If it hadn't been for Tim's accident the hero would still be in the vase now, perched on the mantelpiece; a terrible secret trapped forever.

'Come along dear, keep up,' Tim's mother said as she strode past some hyacinths.

'Can we go home now?' Tim asked, picking up his pace.

'Not yet.'

'But it's cold.' He glanced at the sky. 'And it's starting to rain.'

Mum muttered something under her breath and kept walking.

Tim tried again. 'I'm bored.'

Mum turned and fixed Tim with a penetrating stare. 'We wouldn't be here at all, if it weren't for … well, you know why.' She pressed her lips together and put a tray of petunias in her trolley.

Mum didn't say it out loud but Tim

knew what she meant. If he hadn't destroyed their garden, she wouldn't need to replant it. Except … he hadn't been the one to slash and burn all their flowers. It had been Hercules.

Asking the hero for help with the weeding had turned out to be a big mistake. How was Tim to know that Hercules thought plants had to be fought off like the Hydra, a multi-headed monster whose heads grew back after being sliced off? Hercules was super-strong but not exactly super-smart. Even so, he'd proved to be a loyal friend. He had sided with him against Leo the bully, and encouraged Tim to stand up for himself. Despite all the trouble he'd caused at home and at school,

Tim missed Hercules. There had been no such thing as boredom when the hero was around.

Unlike now.

Sighing, Tim trailed after his mother as she turned yet another corner.

And fell flat on his face.

■ ■ ■

Malicious laughter erupted above him. Tim looked up to see his worst enemy, Leo, looming over him, a grin on his flushed face.

'OOPS! CLUMSY.'

Leo snickered.

Tim knew very well that he'd been tripped over on purpose. He pulled himself to his feet with as much dignity as he could muster.

'What are you doing here, Cinderella?'

Leo used the nickname that he'd made up. It was a cruel dig at the fact that Tim did housework. Not that he wanted to, of course, but Mum worked two jobs and he had to help out. That didn't stop the bully from teasing him about it, however.

'Having fun looking at the flowers, are you? Find anything nice?' Leo pursed his lips in a mock pout and fluttered his eyelashes.

Was it worth pointing out that Leo was at the garden centre too? Tim paused, pondering the best way to put this.

The bully must have misinterpreted

Tim's thoughtful expression for one of fear.

'Go on, go find your mummy,' Leo sneered. 'Maybe she'll buy you a pretty flower so you won't cry.'

Normally Tim would walk away, preferring to avoid trouble rather than tackle it head-on. But since he'd outsmarted Leo once before, he'd grown bolder in their encounters.

'Yeah, I'm just chilling.' Tim folded his arms and ignored the dirt and dead leaves clinging to his trousers. 'But why are *you* here? Have you suddenly become a botanist?'

Leo narrowed his eyes and didn't answer. Tim suspected the bully was

trying to work out what a botanist was,
and whether he'd just been insulted.
Shrugging, Leo pulled a bag of jelly beans
out of his pocket and popped a red one
into his mouth.

Tim's stomach growled at the sight of the food. He hadn't eaten since breakfast and it was nearly lunchtime. He clamped a hand over his gut, hoping Leo hadn't heard.

'Ooh, would ya like one?' Leo patted the bulging bag. 'Sorry, I'm all out.'

'Leo! Where've you got to? Leo!'

The angry voice grew louder. Tim saw a small woman striding towards them, her head darting from side to side like a bird of prey. Her grey hair was pulled back in a severe bun and her eyes flashed behind thick glasses.

'Here, Nan,' Leo called out half-heartedly. He dropped his gaze to the ground.

'Where? Drat the boy. Always wandering off. One of these days I'll …'

'I said here!' Leo turned towards the small figure, a look of misery on his face. 'You're lucky I'm busy,' he shot over his shoulder at Tim. 'Otherwise I'd fix you up.'

Tim hesitated – but only for a moment. Just as Leo started to walk away, Tim put his foot out.

'Oops! Clumsy.' Tim repeated Leo's excuse as the bully fell face first into the dirt.

Leo grunted as he hit the ground, hard. Tim darted off before the bully had a chance to pull himself upright, the words 'I'll fix you up for that, Cinderella!' ringing in his ears.

Tim realised that giving Leo a taste of his own medicine probably wasn't the smartest thing to do, but he knew that Hercules would have been proud. Acting quickly, Tim thrust himself into a group

of chattering old ladies clustered around
a stand of waving sunflowers. Leo would
think twice about following him into their
midst, especially with his nan watching.

Concerned about drawing attention to himself, Tim tried to look interested in the display.

It was the first time he'd ever seen a sunflower up close. Something caught his eye. Its bright yellow head was filled with pointy little seeds. Tim had eaten sunflower seeds many times before as a snack, but had never been bored enough to give them much thought. But now – safe from Leo and with Mum still shopping – he had plenty of time to kill. He peered at the blossom. How exactly did the seeds come out? Did they fall when you shook them? Experimenting, Tim grasped the flower's long stalk and shook it gingerly.

Nothing happened.

He tried a bit harder.

Still nothing.

And a little bit harder …

'Oi! Whaddya think you're doing?'

The voice of a store assistant took Tim by surprise. Startled, he jerked back, snapping the stem clean through.

'YOU CAN'T DO THAT!'

The assistant started
wading through the
crowd of shoppers in Tim's
direction, an angry look on his
face.

With the sunflower still in
his hand, Tim ran the opposite
way. Any minute now the
assistant might call the police

– and then he'd really be in trouble. They wouldn't believe it was an accident. They'd think he was a vandal. Or a thief. Quick, he had to hide the evidence! Panting, Tim scrunched the flower up in his palm and shoved it in his trouser pocket.

'Tim! There you are. Slow down!' Mum wheeled her laden trolley over to him and put her hand on his shoulder. 'Where did you vanish to?'

'Mum. Can we go now? Please.' He tried not to sound frantic.

Mum looked Tim up and down, taking in his wild expression and heaving chest.

'What's up?'

'Nothing. I–'

'Madam, your son has been damaging

store property.' The assistant caught up with them, huffing and puffing, his face redder than the store's roses. He was carrying the pot with the decapitated sunflower.

'Why? What did he do?' Mum gripped Tim's shoulder harder than was necessary.

'This.' The assistant hoisted up the plant. 'I'm afraid you'll have to buy it.'

Mum looked like she was about to argue, but then changed her mind. 'Yes, all right. I'm sorry about that. I'm sure it was an accident.'

The assistant sniffed in disbelief and plunked the severed plant into Mum's trolley. He glared at Tim, then flounced away.

'Would you care to explain that, Timothy?' Mum asked as they joined the queue for the counter. She only called him Timothy when she was cross.

'It was an accident! I was just looking at it. I didn't mean to break it.'

'What is it with you and flowers?'

Tim didn't know what to say.

'At least you didn't set fire to anything,' she said wryly. Tim couldn't tell whether she was joking or not. 'Come on, help me unload the trolley. When we get home I'll make us some lunch. Spaghetti okay?'

Tim's gurgling stomach answered for him.

■ ■ ■

Mum bustled around the kitchen,

cooking and humming a cheerful tune. She'd been in a good mood ever since a publisher had accepted her book – which was probably why Tim wasn't in trouble for breaking the sunflower. Thankfully she'd believed him when he'd said it was an accident. Mum had been busier than ever lately, but she was happy and that made her nicer. Most of the time.

Tugging off his rain-spattered coat, Tim ran into his bedroom to check on the vase. Hercules ought to be happy too, he thought, now that he finally had what he wanted. By solving a tricky riddle printed on the vase, Tim had been able to send the demigod back to his family in Ancient Greece. For the third time that day, Tim

made sure that the vase was still in his wardrobe. He whipped off the sheet that cloaked it and there it was, its fracture lines visible even in the gloomy light.
A few days ago Tim had removed the glued-together vase from the living room mantelpiece and put it where he could keep a close eye on it. Mum didn't seem to mind.

Although he didn't say why, Tim had a very good reason for wanting to keep the vase hidden. Not long after Hercules had left, two intruders had entered Tim's house in the dead of night. They tried to steal the vase from right under Tim's horrified gaze. One was the evil goddess Hera, who wanted to use the vase to recapture Hercules. The other intruder was her servant, a young man called Hermes. He had wings on his cap and sandals and used them to fly. Hermes was clearly terrified of Hera, which only reinforced all of the awful things Hercules had said about her.

Tim had managed to stop them taking the vase, but the flying guy had threatened to return. Tim kept his gaze on the big black vessel as he started to unknot his scarf. Hermes and Hera could come back at any–

'Hey!' Tim yelped, his eyes bulging.

The vase! It was floating!

At first it looked like there was nobody holding it, but Hermes gradually materialised. His body shimmered as it solidified in front of Tim's eyes. The intruder's gaze sharpened when he saw Tim watching him.

'Got it!' Hermes crowed. 'Sweet. Hera will be chuffed.' The wings on his cap and sandals started to flap vigorously and he rose into the air. 'Cheers mate!'

'No-o-o-o!' Without thinking, Tim rushed at the flying figure. He jumped, hands outstretched, and hooked his fingers around the handles.

'HAH!'

But Tim's shout of triumph turned to a cry of fear as he felt himself being lifted off his feet. Higher and higher they went. He was flying! Soon he'd hit the ceiling. Except, somehow they went through it ... A shower of golden sparks danced around his body, thick and fast, blinding him.

Tim shut his eyes and clung on for dear life.

HOPELESS HEROES

To download Hopeless Heroes

ACTIVITIES AND POSTERS

visit
sweetcherrypublishing.com/resources

Sweet Cherry
Publishing